D0904775

WITHDRAWN

-My Family-
My Blended Family

by Claudia Harrington
illustrated by Zoe Persico

Looking Glass Library

An Imprint of Magic Wagon
abdopublishing.com

To Papa for always being a wonderful source of love, smiles, and singing country songs. —ZP

abdopublishing.com

Published by Magic Wagon, a division of ABDO, PO Box 398166, Minneapolis, Minnesota 55439. Copyright © 2018 by Abdo Consulting Group, Inc. International copyrights reserved in all countries. No part of this book may be reproduced in any form without written permission from the publisher. Looking Glass Library™ is a trademark and logo of Magic Wagon.

Printed in the United States of America, North Mankato, Minnesota.
052017
092017

Written by Claudia Harrington
Illustrated by Zoe Persico
Edited by Heidi M.D. Elston
Art Directed by Candice Keimig

Publisher's Cataloging-in-Publication Data

Names: Harrington, Claudia, author. | Persico, Zoe, illustrator.
Title: My blended family / by Claudia Harrington ; illustrated by Zoe Persico.
Description: Minneapolis, MN : Magic Wagon, 2018. | Series: My family
Summary: Lenny follows Olivia for a school project and learns what it's like to be
    part of a blended family.
Identifiers: LCCN 2017930507 | ISBN 9781532130175 (lib. bdg.) |
    ISBN 9781614798323 (ebook) | ISBN 9781614798392 (Read-to-me ebook)
Subjects: LCSH: Family--Juvenile fiction. | Family life--Juvenile fiction. |
    Stepfamilies--Juvenile fiction. | Children of divorced parents--Juvenile fiction.
Classification: DDC [E]--dc23
LC record available at http://lccn.loc.gov/2017930507

"Here, Lenny," said Miss Fish, handing him the camera.

"Olivia is Student of the Week!"

"Hi," they both said.

Click!

"Why is there a flag in your crown?" asked Lenny.

Olivia smiled. "So I can be a princess AND president! Plus, I love costumes."

"Cool," said Lenny. "How do you get home?"

"We have to wait for my sisters, Eve and Tiffany," said Olivia.

A third and fourth grader bounded over, squeezing Olivia. "Olivia sandwich!"

They all cracked up.

Lenny raised his camera.

"And my brothers, Toby and Sam."
Two older boys dribbled in.

"Any more?" asked Lenny.

Olivia grinned. "That's all."

Click!

"Lead the way, president princess," said Sam.

When they slowed, Lenny froze. "You live in the haunted house?"

Click!

Eve and Tiffany elbowed each other as Olivia pulled Lenny through the creaky door.

"It's not haunted," said Olivia. "We just needed something big. Nora agreed to leave the shutters until after Halloween."

Lenny shivered. "Who's Nora?"

"My stepmom," said Olivia.

Lenny's stomach rumbled. "Who gets your snack?"
"We all do," said Olivia. "Watch." Then she turned
and yelled, "SNACKS!"

Olivia passed plates, while Toby flung granola bars. Eve juggled oranges. Tiffany filled waters. And Sam sliced apples.
Click!

"Is it always like a circus?" asked Lenny.

Olivia found a clown nose when they sat at the table. "Usually!"

"Who helps with your homework?" asked Lenny.

"Eve or Tiffany," Olivia said. "They both had Miss Fish."

"Wooooooooooooo," they heard from under the table.

Lenny swallowed. "Who scares away the ghosts?"

Olivia lifted the tablecloth. "No ghosts. Just sisters."

Lenny's cheeks flushed.

"Nora usually tickles them away." Olivia grinned as her stepmom sneaked in.

"Two, four, six . . . When did we get a new one?" Olivia's dad joked as he started spaghetti.

Everybody laughed.

Click!

"Meet my dad and stepmom," said Olivia. "Nora, Dad, this is Lenny."

"Hi," they said. "Homework done?"

"Just choosing Halloween costumes tonight!"
said Olivia, pulling Lenny along.
"I'm going to be a robot!" said Lenny
over his shoulder.

When they got to the attic, Lenny's jaw dropped. "Wow, who got you all these costumes?"

"When Dad married Nora, I got siblings AND all their costumes!"

"How do you decide?" asked Lenny.

Olivia laughed. "I can be them all!" She chose monster gloves, an owl cape, and a NASA cap. **Click!**

Olivia ran to a trunk in the corner of the room. "Want bat wings for your robot?" she asked excitedly.

"Awesome," said Lenny.

A bell clanged, startling Lenny. "What was that?" he asked.

Olivia grinned. "Dad's dinner bell!"

As they sat, rolls flew overhead.

Click!

"Is dinnertime always so crazy?" asked Lenny.

Olivia grinned. "You should see taco night!"

After dinner, Olivia showed Lenny her room. "We girls get upstairs."

Click!

"If Nora and Dad have a baby, WE get it with US!"

Lenny gulped. "Where would it sleep?"

Olivia smiled. "There's always room for one more."

"Who reads you a story?" asked Lenny.

"Nora and Dad take turns," said Olivia as they brought books in.

Outside the door, the stairs creaked.

Lenny froze. "Was that a ghost?"

"Boo!" said Lenny's mom, poking her head in.

"Whew!" said Lenny.

"Who loves you best?" Lenny asked Olivia.

"Us!" said the grown-ups.

Click!

"No way," said Eve. "It's me!"

"And me!" added Tiffany.

Two brother heads poked in, making buzzer sounds. "Wrong answer! It's us!"

Click!

"And me," said Lenny's mom, kissing his head.

Student of the Week

Olivia

"Tomorrow, bat-robot!" said Olivia.

"Tomorrow, monster-owl-astronaut!"
Lenny waved.

32